380 18 0041087 5

D1146667

HIGH

Seaside Escape

HIGHLAND
LIBRARIES

by Cari Meister

illustrated by Heather Burns

raintree 🐾

a Capstone company — publishers for children

WITHDRAWN

Raintree is an imprint of Capstone Global Library Limited, a company incorporated in
England and Wales having its registered office at 264 Banbury Road, Oxford, OX2 7DY –
Registered company number: 6695582

www.raintree.co.uk
myorders@raintree.co.uk

Text © Capstone Global Library Limited 2019
The moral rights of the proprietor have been asserted.

All rights reserved. No part of this publication may be reproduced in any form or by any
means (including photocopying or storing it in any medium by electronic means and
whether or not transiently or incidentally to some other use of this publication) without
the written permission of the copyright owner, except in accordance with the provisions of
the Copyright, Designs and Patents Act 1988 or under the terms of a licence issued by the
Copyright Licensing Agency, Barnard's Inn, 86 Fetter Lane, London, EC4A 1EN (www.cla.
co.uk). Applications for the copyright owner's written permission should be addressed to the
publisher.

Designed by Lori Bye
Original illustrations © Capstone Global Library Limited 2019
Originated by Capstone Global Library Ltd
Printed and bound in India

ISBN 978 1 4747 6272 4
22 21 20 19 18
10 9 8 7 6 5 4 3 2 1

British Library Cataloguing in Publication Data
A full catalogue record for this book is available from the British Library.

Acknowledgements
Design elements by Shutterstock: Semiletava Hanna

CONTENTS

CHAPTER 1

Loading

"In you go, big guy," said Toni the stable manager.

Sebastian was the first to be loaded onto the trailer. He was the biggest horse on Farley Farms. But he never gave anyone trouble. Seb clomped up the ramp. He settled right in, grabbing a mouthful of hay from the hay net.

Snowy, the little Shetland pony, was next. As Toni led him from his stall, there was a commotion at the back of the stable. Riley, the stable dog, was barking loudly.

"What's going on back there?" asked Toni. She left Snowy standing by the door. "Stay there, please," she called back to him.

Of course, this was planned. Snowy needed a distraction so he could grab a few things from his hiding place before they left. Luckily, Riley was easily swayed. All Snowy had to do was tell him he would give him a treat later.

Seb neighed. "Did you get your stuff, Snowy?" he asked.

Snowy quickly rushed up to the trailer and hid a bag under some straw. "Don't call me that," he told Seb. "Please call me by my proper show name!"

"Of course, *The Blizzard*" Seb said. "I'm sorry I forgot."

Snowy nodded and then rushed back to the front of the stable just as Toni came around the corner.

"That silly dog," Toni said. "He was barking at his hedgehog toy!" Toni patted Snowy's neck. "That's odd," she said. "Why are you breathing so heavily? Are you ill? You were just standing here. You shouldn't be puffing. Hmmm . . . I wonder if I should leave you at home."

Snowy rubbed against Toni and nickered. He looked up at her with his big brown eyes. *Please! Please! You just have to take me!* Snowy thought. He tried very hard to relax his breathing.

"Let's take your temperature, just to make sure," Toni said. "I wouldn't want you out on the trail if you were ill. Stand here. I'll get the thermometer."

This time Snowy did not move. His breathing returned to normal.

Toni came back with the thermometer. She lifted his tail. Snowy usually made a fuss when Toni took his temperature, but today he stood very still. He didn't want to risk being left at home.

After a minute, Toni checked the thermometer. "Nope, no temp," she said. "And you seem to be breathing normally. I suppose you can go."

Snowy trotted straight up into the trailer.

"That just leaves Princess," sighed Toni. "I hope loading her doesn't go as badly as last time."

The last time Toni had tried to load Princess, Princess had somehow ended up on top of the trailer.

When Snowy asked her about it later, Princess just licked her long legs.

"Cats like to be up high," she had said.

Then Snowy understood.

Princess – the perfect palomino pony – had always believed she was a cat.

CHAPTER 2

Princess the cat

Toni opened Princess' stall door. Princess pranced in circles.

"Princess," soothed Toni, "be a good horse and let me put your halter on."

Horse! Fumed Princess. *There she goes again. Insisting I am a horse. I am a cat. I have always been a cat. I will always be a cat. I like to chase mice. I like to eat tuna and cheese. Not dry grass! Why does everyone insist that I am a horse? Look at my nice long tail. Look at my big, cunning cat eyes!*

Toni stood patiently waiting until Princess had finished her little dance. She did this every day, so it was nothing new.

But Seb and Snowy were impatient. They wanted to get going. They neighed and nickered to Princess.

"What is taking you so long?" asked Seb.

"It is almost time for *Tres Caballos Incognito!*" said Snowy.

"What does that mean again?" asked Seb.

"It's Spanish for 'three horses in disguise'," explained Snowy. "I have three masks to help hide us on our adventure!"

"Oh yes," said Seb. "I remember now."

"Be a good horse. I mean cat! And let Toni put on your halter," said Snowy.

"I think your friends are ready to go," Toni said to Princess.

Princess' ears perked up. She listened.

"Our adventure awaits!" shouted Snowy.

Oh, that's right! Princess thought. *We are just pretending to go along with Toni, but we are going to escape for an adventure! At least my good friends Seb and Snowy understand me. They know I need to be out in the world as who I am meant to be: Princess: The Feline Wonder.*

Princess walked over to Toni and nosed her hand helping Toni put on her halter.

"Well, that's new!" said Toni. "Perhaps you will actually just walk straight up and into the trailer too?"

And Princess did.

CHAPTER 3

A plan

"So what is our adventure today?" asked Princess as the truck and trailer pulled away.

"I'm not sure," said Snowy. "Seb, do you have any ideas?"

Seb wasn't paying attention. They were going past Ravenscraft Farm. Betty lived there. Betty was a shire horse, like him. Seb loved her with all his heart. But he had never had the courage to tell her.

Maybe I will shout it out as we drive by, Seb thought to himself.

But as they neared her pasture, Betty wasn't there.

Seb did a double-take. Where was she? She was always there. She lived outside.

Princess noticed that Seb was upset. "Betty's moved," she told him.

"Moved?" asked Seb. "Where?"

Princess pushed out her legs in front of her and stretched. "Not sure exactly. Somewhere far away. I think she had to fly there."

"Fly there?" asked Seb. "She's left the country?"

"Something like that," said Princess. "That's what Toni was saying the other day."

Seb's whole body sunk. "How can this be?" he sobbed. "I loved her, you know. Now I will never see her again! And I never even told her that I loved her."

"There, there," said Snowy. "I think she knew."

"Really?" asked Seb.

"I'm sure of it," said Princess. "How could she not? Think of all those times you sat in the corner of your pasture and sang love songs in her direction. And the times you managed to sneak over and give her your best alfalfa hay."

Snowy nodded and said, "She knew."

But that didn't make Seb feel any better.

"Now she's gone!" he said. "And I will never see her again."

"Don't worry," said Snowy. "You know what they say."

"No," said Seb. "What do they say?"

"There are plenty of fish in the sea," said Snowy.

"There are?" asked Princess dancing in place. "I've always wanted to catch fish!"

"That's not what I meant," said Snowy.

"Still," said Princess, "can we go to the sea? I want to catch fish!"

Snowy rummaged through the bag he had hidden under the straw. He picked up a hoof pick in his mouth, opened his laptop and typed in: remote seaside beaches near me.

He looked up at his friends. "We're in luck!" he said. "There is a beach not too far from where Toni is taking us for the – ahem – trail ride."

"That we are not going on!" shouted Princess.

"What's the beach called?" asked Seb.

Snowy looked down at the screen and squinted. "It's called *Lonely Man's Paradise*."

Princess crinkled her nose. "Do you think it will have fish?"

"Absolutely," said Snowy.

"I've always wanted to swim in the sea," said Seb.

"Then its purrrrrfect!" said Princess.

CHAPTER 4

The escape

The trailer rumbled on for another hour or so until Toni pulled into a petrol station.

Snowy looked at the map on his laptop.

"This is our chance," he said. "When Toni goes inside to pay, we escape!"

"Let's see those *Tres Caballos Incognito masks*," said Princess.

"Of course," said Snowy pulling out three special fly masks they always wore for adventures.

Snowy turned to ask Seb to start working on the door latch, but Seb had it under control. The back was already open.

Princess stuck her head through the trailer bars. "I can see Toni," she said. "She's going in now."

The three friends trotted down the ramp. Then Seb carefully closed it.

"Hurry!" said Snowy. "We don't want to get caught."

"Let's hide," said Princess.

By the time Toni was back in the truck, the three friends had hidden behind a tree. Luckily, Toni wasn't looking their way.

As the truck and empty trailer drove away, Snowy looked at the map. "I think it's best if we don't take the road," he said. "Less chance that we will be caught."

"Fine with me," said Princess. "After all, a cat likes to remain in the shadows. It's more mysterious."

"Seb?" asked Snowy.

Seb was just staring into the distance thinking about Betty. "Whatever," he said.

So the three friends made their own path, heading to the beach.

In the meantime, Toni had started up the truck. As she drove away, something seemed wrong. "That's strange," she mumbled to herself. "The trailer seems to be pulling much more easily now."

Toni just shrugged and kept on driving.

CHAPTER 5

Stuck!

It was a long way to the beach.

"I need to rest," huffed Snowy after about an hour. "I'm not used to this much exercise."

"I'm going to hunt," said Princess.

"Don't go far," said Snowy. "And don't get stuck in a tree again."

Princess snorted. "That was an accident," she replied.

"I know," said Snowy. "It would be disappointing if we had to get Toni to rescue you."

Remembering the time when Princess got stuck in the tree made Seb smile a little.

"That's the spirit," said Snowy. "It reminds me of a quote I once read: "A smile is happiness you'll find right under your nose."

Seb grunted and started grazing.

"I heard the funniest joke the other day," Snowy said, determined to make the adventure a good one for his sad friend. "It goes like this: A horse walks into a restaurant. The waiter looks at him and asks, "Why the long face?""

Snowy stamped the grass and chuckled. "Funny, huh?" he asked.

Seb looked down at Snowy and replied, "Is that the best you can do?"

Snowy frowned at his friend. He had hoped to cheer up Seb, but it wasn't working. He leaned over and opened his laptop.

Snowy had been working on his novel, *From the Horse's Mouth*, for quite some time, but it was far from being finished. Snowy typed:

```
Our hero found himself unsure of what
to do next. Although he was having a
wonderful time, his dear friend was not.
And when one is happy and the other is
sad, joy vanishes. Our hero tried a
joke, but it fell flat. So for now, he
was hoping just being there was enough
for his suffering fri—
```

"MIIAAAOOWW-HELP!"

Seb and Snowy looked at each other.

"Oh no," said Snowy. "What do you think she's done *this* time?"

"We'd better go and look," said Seb.

***

When Seb and Snowy got to Princess they both burst out laughing.

Princess was in someone's back garden. Her back legs were in a sandpit. Her front legs were through a playhouse ladder. And her head was 100 per cent stuck in the playhouse window.

"I can't move!" she cried.

"What happened?" asked Snowy.

"I was chasing another cat," explained Princess. "I wanted to be friends, so I just followed him through the sandpit. Then he went up the ladder and through the window, but I got stuck."

"I think you must be a bit bigger than that cat," said Seb.

"He was rather small," said Princess, trying to pull her head out. "Can you help?"

Snowy thought about it. "I think if Seb goes under you, you will be able to get your front legs out," he said. "Then you can stand on him and use your weight to pull your head back. I will help push."

It took five tries, but finally Princess was standing on Seb.

"You are one heavy kitty," Seb grumbled.

"I think your hooves – I mean paws – may leave marks on my coat."

But Princess was not listening. She was starting to panic.

"It's okay," said Snowy. "Don't worry. We will get you out."

"Are you sure?" asked Princess. "I am super stuck! What if I have to stay here forever?"

Snowy climbed up the slide from the other side of the playhouse and was soon facing Princess.

"OK, on three. Seb, you stand still, Princess you pull. I will push from this side," said Snowy. "One, two, three!"

And just like that, Princess' head was out. "Thank you!" she cried. "Now let's go and catch some fish!"

CHAPTER 6

The sea

After another twenty minutes of walking, Snowy lifted his head.

He inhaled deeply. "AHHH!" he said.

"We are close. I can smell the sea."

Princess and Seb stopped and lifted their heads too. They inhaled.

"That's the smell of the sea?" asked Princess.

"Yes," said Snowy.

"It smells wet, salty and wonderful!" said Seb.

Seb broke into a trot. Princess and Snowy followed.

Their hooves hitting the sand felt glorious.

Sebastian took it all in: The waves crashing. The birds swooping. And two beautiful mares prancing by the water's edge–

Seb shook his head and looked again. But the mares were gone.

He turned to his friends. "Did you see two mares down by the crashing waves a second ago?" he asked.

Snowy and Princess looked at the sea and shook their heads.

"Maybe it was a mirage," said Snowy. "A vision."

Seb looked again. No prancing mares.

"Or maybe they were hippocampi," said Snowy.

"Hippo-what?" asked Princess.

"Hippocampi – plural for Hippocampus. A Hippocampus is a water horse. It is a creature from Greek mythology," said Snowy.

"Are they real?" asked Seb.

Snowy shrugged. "Who's to say? Scientists are discovering new creatures in the sea all the time. They say the ocean is largely unexplored. Unknown creatures live down there. So who knows?"

That was all the explanation Seb needed. He bolted for the sea, looking for love.

Princess turned to Snowy. "How do I catch fish without getting wet?" she asked. "You know, some cats hate water."

"And we don't have any fishing rods," said Snowy.

"Ha!" said Princess. "That would be funny! A cat fishing with a fishing rod. *Really*, Snowy, have some common sense!"

Snowy tried not to laugh. He nodded towards a long pier and said, "Perhaps you could try lying on the pier and catching them with your mouth?"

"Now that sounds reasonable," said Princess. "Would you like to come?"

"No thanks," said Snowy. "I think I will sit here and work on my book, but see if you can catch an extra fish to bring back for Riley. I promised him a treat."

"Absolutely," said Princess as she pranced down to the pier.

CHAPTER 7

Panic at sea

Seb swam back and forth. He swam out and back. He nickered and neighed. He ran along the shoreline. "Hippocampi," he called. "Come back, I just want to see your beautiful manes. I want to see your long flowing tails and shiny coats."

Princess tried to catch fish. First she swatted at the water with her hoof – ahem – her paw. That didn't seem to work. Then, she sprawled out on the pier. She watched the water for hours.

"I can see the fish!" she would call every once in a while. "They are there! I'm just not sure how to get them." Then she would go back to watching the water. Every so often, her head would zip back and forth. She was loving every minute of it.

Snowy sat and typed:

```
The hippocampi surrounded the lovesick
one. They groomed his mane. They brought
him seaweed to eat. As Our Hero watched
his friend, he realized that sometimes
distractions are necessary. They help one
get out of one's own mind and thinking
about different thi—
```

Snowy stopped typing and looked up. Seb was far, far, out to sea. His friend was in danger!

"SEBASTIAN!" called Snowy. "Turn around! Come back!"

Sebastian turned and panicked. He hadn't realized he was out so far.

His long legs splashed in the water. "HELP!" He said. "Help me!"

To Snowy's surprise, Princess jumped off the pier. She swam to Seb's side.

"You are OK," she purred. "You can do this. Relax."

But Seb couldn't relax. His legs slapped at the water. He had a look of terror in his eyes.

"I'm coming!" said Snowy.

Snowy trotted out to the water. He had swum in the ocean before, but it had been a long time ago. He put his front hooves in the crashing waves. Then he went forward. It was just as he remembered – but better. He swam, but his friends were so far away. He couldn't get to Seb to help him.

"Seb," said Princess. "I know you can do this. Think of yourself as a jaguar. Wild jaguars are fantastic swimmers. They swim for fun. Don't worry. I'm right here. I won't let anything happen to you."

So Seb imagined he was a jaguar.

It worked!

Soon Seb and Princess made it back to the beach.

Snowy joined them.

"That was very brave, Princess!" said Snowy.

"Yes, it was," said Seb. "Thank you for rescuing me."

Princess shrugged. "No big deal," she said. "That's what friends do."

The three friends spent the rest of the afternoon building sandcastles and playing in the waves.

The sun was just starting to set as they trotted out of the water and shook off.

"It's getting late," said Seb.

"I didn't catch any fish," said Princess. "I am starving."

"I bet Toni is worried," said Snowy. "We should probably go home, but first we need to find something to take back for Riley."

Snowy nosed the sand until he found something. It was long and reddish.

"What is it?" asked Seb.

Snowy looked closer. "I think it is a piece of a crab's leg," he said.

"It's purrfect," said Princess. "Riley will love it!"

CHAPTER 8

A selfie

Seb and Princess started galloping towards home.

"Wait!" called Snowy. "Not so fast. I have small legs!"

"Sorry, *The Blizzard,*" said Seb. "Sometimes I forget."

The three walked at Snowy's pace for what seemed like hours.

"We will never make it home!" said Princess.

"Do you have any ideas?" asked Seb.

Snowy slumped down on the ground.
He pulled out his laptop.

"This is no time to write," said Princess.
"We have to gooooo!"

Snowy found a social media horse site
that he knew Toni used.

Seb looked over his shoulder. "What are
you doing?" he asked.

"Posting a message," said Snowy. "Come here. I need to take a picture of us."

Seb and Princess came closer. Snowy posed with them. The laptop took a picture of *Tres Caballos Incognito*. He uploaded it to his post. He typed:

```
Three horses sighted near Lonely Man's
Beach: a tall shire horse, a beautiful
show pony and a distinguished looking,
mature Shetland pony.
```

"Now what?" asked Seb.

"Now we wait," said Snowy. "I am guessing Toni will be here in no time."

***

And Snowy was right. It didn't take long for Toni to find them.

"What on earth?" she asked when she arrived. "How did you get out? And what is going on with these masks?"

Toni loaded the horses onto the trailer.

Seb and Princess fell fast asleep after a few minutes. Snowy watched them. Seb was leaning against the side of the trailer. His eyes were closed, but he had a giant smile on his face.

Seb mumbled something about "more fish in the sea".

Princess' mouth was snapping and lunging.

Snowy laughed. *She's still fishing*, he thought to himself. *I hope she catches a fish in her dreams.*

Snowy opened up his laptop. He typed in one last thing:

"Our hoofbeats were many, our hearts beat as one." Anonymous

He closed his eyes and fell into a deep sleep, dreaming of another adventure for *Tres Caballos Incognito*.

GLOSSARY

alfalfa type of grass

commotion lots of noisy, excited activity

cunning clever

distinguished noted for the important things that a person has done

feline any animal of the cat family

glorious wonderful, beautiful

graze eat grass that is growing in a field

impatient in a hurry and unable to wait

inhale breathe in

mature older or more sensible

mirage something that you think you can see in the distance, but that is not really there

mumble speak quietly and unclearly, with the mouth half closed

panic sudden feeling of great fear

pier platform that extends over a body of water

rummage look for something by moving things around in an untidy or careless way

swayed changed or influenced how someone thinks or behaves

terror very great fear

ABOUT THE AUTHOR

Cari Meister has written more than 130 books for children, including the Tiny series (Penguin) and the Fast Forward Fairy Tales series (Scholastic). Cari is a school librarian and she loves to visit other schools and libraries to talk about the joy of reading and writing. Cari lives in the mountains of Colorado, USA, with her husband, four boys, one horse and one dog.

ABOUT THE ILLUSTRATOR

Heather Burns is an illustrator from Uttoxeter, UK. In 2013, she graduated from the University of Lincoln with a degree in illustration and has been working as a freelance illustrator ever since. Heather has a passion for bringing stories to life with pictures and hopes that her work makes people smile. When she's not working she's usually out walking her grumpy black Labrador, Meadow!

TALK ABOUT IT

1. List three moments in the story where *Tres Caballos Incognito* behaved as good friends towards one another.

2. Do you think Riley will like the gift *Tres Caballos Incognito* found for him?

3. Why do you think Princess is always difficult when Toni tries to load her into the trailer?

WRITE ABOUT IT

1. Pretend you're Toni. Make a "Missing Horses" flyer for *Tres Caballos Incognito*.

2. Seb panics in the sea. Write about a time when you were very afraid. What did you do?

3. Write a scene where Toni arrives at her destination and discovers the horses are missing. What is going through her mind?

BOOKS IN THE THREE HORSES SERIES

THE FUN DOESN'T STOP HERE!

Discover more at www.raintree.co.uk